A WOODLAND MYSTERY™

The Mystery of the Missing Dog

A WOODLAND MYSTERY
By Irene Schultz

The Wright Group®

To Jonathan, Tony, and Mark Hofeld, my own Woodland family of rascally boys

The Mystery of the Missing Dog
©1996 Wright Group Publishing, Inc.
©1996 Story by Irene Schultz
Cover and cameo illustrations by Taylor Bruce
Interior illustrations by Meredith Yasui
Map illustration by Alicia Kramer

Woodland Mysteries™
© Wright Group Publishing, Inc.

The Woodland Mysteries were created by the
Wright Group development team.

The Wright Group
19201 120th Avenue NE
Bothell, WA 98011

Printed in the United States of America

10 9 8 7 6 5 4 3

ISBN: 0-7802-7231-5

What family solves mysteries...has adventures all over the world...and loves oatmeal cookies?

It's the Woodlanders!

Sammy Westburg (10 years old)
His sister Kathy Westburg (13)
His brother Bill Westburg (14)
His best friend Dave Briggs (16)
His best grown-up friend Mrs. Tandy
And Mop, their little dog!

The children all lost their parents, but with Mrs. Tandy have made their own family.

Why are they called the Woodlanders? Because they live in a big house in the Bluff Lake woods. On Woodland Street!

Together they find fun, mystery, and adventure. What are they up to now?

Read on!

Meet the Woodlanders!

Sammy Westburg
Sammy is a ten-year-old wonder! He's big for his fifth-grade class, and big-mouthed, too. He has wild hair and makes awful spider faces. Even so, you can't help liking him.

Bill Westburg
Bill, fourteen, is friendly and strong, and only one inch taller than his brother Sammy. He loves Sammy, but pokes him to make him be quiet! He's in junior high.

Kathy Westburg
Kathy, thirteen, is small, shy, and smart. She wants to be a doctor someday! She loves to be with Dave, and her brothers kid her about it. She's in junior high, too.

Dave Briggs

Dave, sixteen, is tall and blond. He can't walk, so he uses a wheelchair and drives a special car. He likes coaching high-school sports, solving mysteries, and reading. And Kathy!

Mrs. Tandy

Sometimes the kids call her Mrs. T. She's Becky Tandy, their tall, thin, caring friend. She's always ready for a new adventure, and for making cookies!

Mop

Mop is the family's little tan dog. Sometimes they have to leave him behind with friends. But he'd much rather be running after Sammy.

Table of Contents

Chapter   **Page**

1   The Surprise at the Ranch 1

2   Fun in the Snow 9

3   Where's Dusty? 19

4   Trapped 27

5   The Rescue..35

6   Skin and Bones 45

7   Sheriff Garza 55

8   Tennessee Turner..............................65

9   The Missing Cabin 75

10 Space Monsters 83

11 Big! And Fat! And Hairy! 93

12 A Party 103

13 The Last Trap 111

Chapter 1:
The Surprise at the Ranch

"Hey!" yelled ten-year-old Sammy Westburg. "A DEER!"

He hit his brother's leg and pointed out the car window.

The deer leaped lightly across a snowy field. It disappeared into the pine woods.

The over-sized station wagon bumped along slowly. Everything was covered with snow, even the road. Abe Adams was driving the five Woodlanders to his family's Montana place, Big Rock River Ranch.

Sammy was sitting in the back with his fourteen-year-old brother Bill and Mrs. Tandy.

Sammy's sister Kathy, thirteen, rode in front with Dave Briggs, their sixteen-year-old friend.

Dave said, "I wish I could drive. I love driving in the snow. Too bad this car doesn't have hand controls!"

Mr. Adams said, "Wait till you see the surprise waiting for you all at the ranch, Dave! You won't miss your car at all."

Sammy said, "Why? What's the surprise?"

Mr. Adams said, "You'll find out as soon as we get there!"

Mrs. Tandy said, "I think just getting to your ranch will be a surprise, Abe. My lands, I never saw so much snow. And here it is, almost April!"

Kathy said, "Just think. Back home the snow's almost gone."

Sammy growled, "This is SOME place to spend spring vacation. I brought my

marbles. But I'll have to play with them on skis!"

Bill poked him. He whispered, "Be quiet. You'll make Mr. Adams feel bad. And Mr. Adams is Dave's history teacher back home!"

Sammy yelled, "Stop poking me! I was only kidding! I LOVE snow. I'll prove it!"

He opened the car window a little.

He grabbed some snow that was stuck to the side of the car.

He mashed it onto Bill's cheek.

That was too much for Bill.

4

With one side move, he sat on Sammy.

Finally Sammy said, "OK, OK. Get off me. I give up."

Bill said, "And what else?"

Sammy said, "And I'm sorry about the snow ... and I won't do it again."

Bill moved off of him.

"... until tomorrow," Sammy added.

Then he said, "So let's get back to important business. What's waiting at the ranch that's so great?"

Mr. Adams laughed. "I see you're dying to know. So let's play Twenty Questions. I'll tell you if you guess it right."

Sammy piped right up, "How big is it?"

Dave said, "You have to ask yes-or-no questions, Sammy. Mr. Adams can only answer YES or NO or PARTLY in Twenty Questions."

So Sammy said, "Is it as big as a car?"

Mr. Adams said no.

Mrs. Tandy said, "Is it alive?"

Mr. Adams shook his head. He said, "Nope!"

Dave asked, "Is it made of metal?"

"Partly," Mr. Adams answered.

Kathy asked shyly, "Is it made for having fun?"

Mr. Adams smiled. "Partly!"

Bill said, "I know! Is it some kind of sled?"

Once more, Mr. Adams answered, "Partly."

Sammy said, "How could something be only partly a sled? I give up!"

Bill said, "Don't give up yet!"

But just then they came to the ranch's guest cabins.

Mr. Adams drove right past them.

He said, "You're staying in the house with Ella and me. The cabins aren't heated, and we have plenty of room."

He drove around to the back of his house.

He pointed and said, "There's the surprise! And there are two more of them in the shed!"

Chapter 2:
Fun in the Snow

Their eyes almost popped out of their heads!

All together they shouted, "Snowmobiles!"

Sammy leaped out of the car.

He yelled, "Let's drive them right now!"

He climbed onto the snowmobile and patted the seat behind him.

He said, "Come on, Mr. Adams! I learn fast! Teach me, and I can teach the slowpokes tomorrow!"

Mr. Adams laughed. "Can't. The keys are in the house. Anyway, the sun's going behind the mountain soon. Besides, it's time for dinner!"

Bill called, "Come on, Sammy, let's get our bags inside."

Kathy took Dave's wheelchair out of the car.

Dave pulled himself into it.

Sammy picked up three suitcases at once. He ran toward the back door.

He shouted, "Come on, guys! Let's eat! We have to build up strength for

10

snowmobiling tomorrow!"

Inside the big ranch kitchen, Mrs. Adams hugged them all. She said, "Welcome back! I'm so glad to see you! Come in and make yourselves at home!"

The room was much more than a kitchen. It had a dining table and chairs, and a couch on each end.

Mrs. Adams pointed to two doors. She said, "Those rooms are for you. One for you men and one for the women. Kathy and Becky, put your bags in there, that's right.

11

"Now come into the kitchen and let's eat!"

She put a big bowl of hot noodles on the kitchen table.

Mr. Adams brought over a huge platter.

He said, "There are four different meats here. See, in four piles. Be sure to take some from each pile!"

Sammy filled his plate with meat. He took some noodles and gravy.

Then he asked, "What are we eating? Chicken, beef, pork, and lamb?"

Mr. Adams said, "Nope. These are meats from the freezer, from my hunting. It's rabbit, deer, elk, and bear!"

Sammy said, "Rabbit? Rabbit! You want me to eat some cute little rabbit? And a beautiful deer? Yuck!"

He pushed his plate away.

He sounded so rude, Kathy turned bright pink.

Mrs. Tandy said, "Oh, dear, Sammy. I guess we won't be eating spareribs or hamburgers anymore, then.

"I guess you wouldn't want to eat some cute little pig ... or some sweet old cow, either."

Bill said, "That's OK, Sammy. Here, I can just take your plate. Don't worry, it won't go to waste."

Sammy grabbed the plate back. "Keep your paws off my food, Bill. If YOU want it, then I want it!"

He took a bite. Then he ate it all.

The next morning, Bill was the first one up. He shook Sammy and Dave awake.

Then he tapped on the wall. He heard a tap coming back from the next room. Kathy and Mrs. Tandy were up, too.

Dave got himself into his chair.

But Sammy rolled over, face down. He said, "Go away. Let me sleep."

In a loud voice, Dave said, "Well, Bill. I guess the snowmobiles are all ours!"

In one jump Sammy was out of bed and pulling on his clothes.

He shouted, "Race you getting dressed!"

He had slept in his T-shirt and underwear.

He pulled on his long underwear.

Bill said, "You've got that on backward, Sammy."

Sammy said, "So what?"

Then he threw on a sweatshirt. It went on inside out.

He pulled on his jeans.

He looked in a drawer for his wool socks. He couldn't find them. He grabbed Bill's, right out of his hand.

He stuffed his feet into them. Then he hit Bill with a pillow and yelled, "I beat you getting dressed! I'm the winner!"

His hair stuck out. He was a mess.

But he WAS ready first.

In ten minutes everybody went outside. The three snowmobiles were out and ready to go.

Mrs. Adams said, "Come on, let's go! As soon as you've figured these out, we can have breakfast!"

Mr. Adams pointed to one snowmobile.

He said, "Look at this one, Dave. You remember Ed, the caretaker? Well, he and I built the seat up, front and back, just for you.

"And we added padded sides. And leg holders. You can lower your legs in and stay put."

He handed helmets and ski masks around to everyone. "You have to wear a helmet any time you're riding.

"And don't get wild. Tipping over can kill you!"

Bill said, "We promise. Wow! Look at these things! Tank treads on the back. Skis in the front."

Mr. Adams said, "The skis aim the snowmobile. The treads drive it along. Now let's start with Sammy, Dave, and Kathy."

Bill helped Dave get onto his snowmobile.

Mr. Adams went on. "Steering these is pretty much like steering a bike."

Dave asked, "What are these lever things on the handlebars?"

Mr. Adams said, "The one on the right is the gas. The one on the left is the brakes. Squeeze them to make them work."

Mr. Adams got on behind Sammy.

Mrs. Adams rode with Kathy.

They drove round and round in the snow near the house.

Then Bill and Mrs. Tandy took turns.

In half an hour, Mr. Adams said, "Well, you're all doing fine.

"Now, after breakfast, you can head up the mountain! But you've got to promise to stick together.

"Because you'll be on your own!"

Chapter 3:
Where's Dusty?

They hurried inside to fix breakfast.

Hardly anyone talked. They wanted
to get to those snowmobiles!

But suddenly Kathy said, "Hey, where's

your big old dog? Where's Dusty? He was here last summer."

Dave said, "That's right! We haven't even heard him bark. Is he staying with Ed in the caretaker's cabin?"

Mr. and Mrs. Adams looked at each other sadly.

Mrs. Adams said, "We only wish we could tell you where he is."

Mr. Adams said, "Last month Ed let Dusty out for a run in the snow. Dusty never came back.

"Ed doesn't know if Dusty ran away, or was hit by a car, or was stolen, or got lost, or what."

Mrs. Adams nodded.

She said, "Ed phoned the other ranchers. No one's seen hide nor hair of a gold-and-white collie. And we looked everywhere, too, when we got here."

Mrs. Tandy shook her head. "I'm so

sorry, Ella. He was such a good dog."

Sammy said, "Remember how he used to follow the horses all the time?"

Mrs. Adams smiled. "That's how he got his name. He'd come home with his tongue hanging out. And he'd be all covered with dust."

Bill said, "Remember how he'd jump into the river to get cool ... and then shake off all over Sammy?"

Sammy said, "I didn't care. He was the best!"

Suddenly Dave said, "Look, a dog like Dusty doesn't just run away. There must be some other reason why he's gone."

Kathy said, "Well ... I was thinking that ... "

Sammy said, "What, Kathy? Come on, tell us. We won't laugh, I promise."

Kathy said, "Well, Dusty DID love following the horses to the mountain

meadows.   Remember how he used to chase deer up there?

"What if he thought of going up there alone?

"We could snowmobile up the mountain.   We could see if he left any tracks in the snow up there."

Sammy laughed.   Loud.

Bill said, "Cut it out, Sammy!   You said you wouldn't laugh!   Besides, it's not funny."

Sammy said, "But that's SO stupid! There's been snow since Dusty disappeared.   His tracks would be covered up. It even snowed yesterday!"

Mr. Adams said, "Not so fast, Sammy. It snowed lower down, on the way from the airport.

"Now, I don't know why, but here and above us, it's hardly snowed in a month.

"There just might be some signs of Dusty, higher on the mountainside."

Sammy said, "Well ... that's just what I was going to say. Kathy's idea wasn't so bad. So what are we waiting for? Let's get going!"

Mr. Adams turned to Mrs. Tandy and said, "OK, then, Becky! You and Sammy take one snowmobile.

"Kathy and Bill, take another.

"Dave, you're fine alone.

"Now, you all have a good time. And don't be too disappointed if you can't find anything. See you around noon!"

He handed a candy bar to each of them. He said, "These will help you keep warm!"

They headed outside, helped Dave onto his snowmobile, climbed aboard, and

drove off.

Sammy and Kathy had first turns driving. Mrs. Tandy and Bill sat in back of them and held on.

Dave led the way over snow two feet deep. He took a path that zig-zagged up the mountain.

The wind blew cold but their ski masks kept their faces warm.

They watched on both sides for dog tracks in the snow.

They drove past steep drop-offs and through thick pine woods.

At 10:30 Dave stopped his snowmobile.

24

He said, "It's almost time to turn around and start back. We have to go down slowly to be safe."

Bill said, "First let's turn off our motors, and sit here for a minute. I want to get a good look from up here."

He pointed. "It all looks so different than it did last summer."

Mrs. Tandy said, "Say, it's lucky we stopped. It's time to change drivers!"

Sammy said, "ROTTEN RATS! I was hoping you'd forget."

But he turned off his motor.

Kathy turned hers off, too.

She said, "Doesn't everything look beautiful?

"Nothing but the dark green pines ... and the tiny-looking ranch buildings ... and the silver thread of a river ... and the white snow all over.

"And not a sound but the wind."

25

They stood looking at the snowy land below them.

Bill pointed out a hawk sailing through the still, cold air.

He whispered, "Probably after a rabbit."

Suddenly, from far off, a faint noise broke through the air.

Bill said, "My gosh! Do you hear what I hear?"

The others stared, with their mouths hanging open.

From someplace on the mountain the sound came again.

It was the bark of a dog.

Chapter 4:
Trapped

"DUSTY!" they all said at once.

Their voices sounded loud in the quiet around them.

Dave said, "Shh ... everyone. Keep

quiet and listen carefully. We have to figure out where that bark came from."

Kathy said, "I think it's coming from up here somewhere."

They all sat quietly.

A minute passed.

Another minute went by.

They heard nothing.

At last Mrs. Tandy said, "Now what do we do?"

Sammy said, "How could it be Dusty, anyway? A dog couldn't stay on a cold mountain by itself and still be alive a month later!

"What would it eat?"

Kathy said, "Maybe it was just a dog on the road down below. Maybe when he barked we heard the echo up here."

Sammy said, "It didn't sound like an echo. What if it IS Dusty? Maybe someone up here is holding him prisoner!"

Bill said, "Oh, come on, Sammy! No one with any brains would be up on this mountain in the snow."

Sammy said, "That would explain what YOU'RE doing here. No brains!"

Bill said, "I mean, who would be staying up here?"

Mrs. Tandy said, "I don't know, but we can't just go back down. We have to look around, in case it WAS Dusty."

Dave nodded. "It's ten thirty-five. It will take an hour or more to get back down. That still gives us a little time to look around.

"So where do you guys think the sound came from?"

Sammy said, "Further south. Across the front of this mountain."

Bill said, "I thought it came from the south, a little higher than the trail."

Kathy nodded. "I thought it was a

little lower."

Mrs. Tandy said, "Well, anyway, we all think it came from the south."

Dave said, "Then here's the plan. We keep going south, across the mountain. Bill, Kathy, and I will keep our eyes on the land to the left, below.

"Sammy and Mrs. Tandy, you keep a lookout above us."

Sammy said, "Let's go. Now I'm glad it's your turn to drive, Mrs. T. I'm GREAT at looking for things."

They started out. After five minutes Dave stopped. They turned off their motors again. They listened.

Nothing.

Bill called out, "Dusty! Oh, Dusty!"

Nothing.

Sammy said, "It's so quiet I can hear my stomach growl. I'm getting hungry!"

He grabbed the candy bar from his

pocket. He munched it down in a minute, right through his ski mask.

Then Bill said, "Sammy, quit munching and listen! Did you hear that?"

But no one else heard what Bill heard.

They sat quietly, listening.

Bill said, "I KNOW I heard a noise. Not a bark. More like a whine. Let's go!"

They started along the trail again.

In another five minutes they stopped. Then they all heard it ... first a whining sound, then a bark!

Dave said, "Come on, guys!" He led them uphill, through a deep woods.

On the other side they came into a snowy meadow.

It was Kathy who cried out, "LOOK! THERE!"

She pointed to a clearing a little below them.

They saw a sight that almost made them cry.

Two animals lay on the ground.

They were both near each other, caught in traps.

A heavy chain held each trap to a stake in the ground.

One of the animals was a deer, or what was left of a deer. It had been ripped open and almost eaten up.

The other animal lay on its side, on a bare circle of ground. It had eaten the snow around it as far as it could reach.

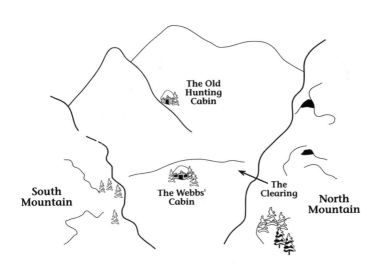

The Old Hunting Cabin

South Mountain

The Webbs' Cabin

The Clearing

North Mountain

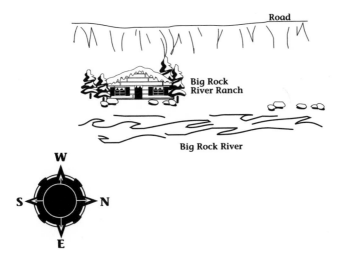

Road

Big Rock River Ranch

Big Rock River

W

S

N

E

Its left hind leg was held in the trap. The animal hardly moved, but its eyes were open.

It was so skinny, it looked almost dead. Its head was so thin, it looked like a skull.

Its fur was matted and dirty, but the Woodlanders could make out its gold-and-white markings.

Slowly, slowly, it lifted its head to look at them.

Dusty!

They had found Dusty!

Chapter 5:
The Rescue

Sammy jumped off his snowmobile.

He ripped off his helmet and ski mask.

He was crying.

He called out, "Here we come, Dusty!"
He started down into the clearing.

But Bill tackled him from behind like
a football player.

Sammy landed face down in the snow.
He turned and started hitting Bill.

Bill said, "Cut it out, Sammy. I HAD
to stop you. You can't just run down
there. There might be another trap
under the snow!"

Dave shouted, "Bill's right, Sammy! We have to get help! We have to go get Mr. Adams! And some shovels!"

Sammy shouted at Bill, "Get your hands off me! I'm not going!

"Dusty might give up and die if we leave him now! He wouldn't know we were coming back!"

Bill said, "Listen, Sammy. We can't split up. We promised Mr. Adams we would stick together.

"And sure, doing it alone we could try to keep ourselves out of other traps. And maybe we would.

"But shovels would make it faster and safer. We could dig a path with them, to spring any other traps."

Dave said, "We don't even know for sure how to open that trap. Maybe we couldn't even get Dusty's leg out of it, without Mr. Adams."

37

Kathy said, "And I guess there's the chance that when we move him, he might go into shock. We'd need something warm to wrap him in.

"And we'd have to muzzle him. He might go wild with pain, and try to bite us when we moved him.

"So maybe Bill's right ... maybe we do need Mr. Adams."

Sammy half-cried, half-yelled, "Well, if I were Dusty, I'd want us to try to get me out! I wouldn't want us to go away and leave me! Look at him there!"

Then Sammy blew his nose so hard, he sounded like a tuba.

Everybody looked at Sammy's tear-covered face.

They looked at Dusty.

Kathy burst out, "Do you know what? Sammy's right! Every word we said makes sense, but still, Sammy's right!"

Dave said, "I don't really want to leave Dusty, either. Sammy IS right!"

Bill said, "I think he is, too."

Mrs. Tandy jumped off her snowmobile. She ran over to Sammy and hugged him ... tears, runny nose, and all.

She said, "There's an old saying ... one person who's right can be as strong as a crowd. That's you, Sammy. But now what do we do?"

Dave called from his snowmobile, "First, you have to get to Dusty safely.

"There were some broken pine branches lying in the snow back there. You know, back in the woods.

"Get some of the big, heavy ones.

"Then walk toward Dusty. Use the branches to test the snow in front of you. You have to spring any traps that might be hidden."

The others ran to the woods. They came back with branches.

They beat the snow flat. They made a wide, safe path.

At last they reached Dusty.

Dave called down to them, "Next we have to figure out how to open that trap. We have to free him.

"But first, what can you do to keep him from biting?"

Mrs. Tandy said, "I'm wearing a silk

scarf inside my coat. We can use it for a muzzle."

She reached inside her coat and brought out the scarf.

Kathy took it and walked up to the waiting dog.

Dusty whined at her, but stopped when she said his name.

Gently she made a muzzle with the scarf. The dog was too weak to fight her.

Sammy, Bill, and Mrs. Tandy were already trying to open the trap.

Dave called, "I've read that some traps have metal bars. Does that one?"

Bill called back, "Yep, I see it."

Dave said, "Then step on the bar hard, and see if the trap opens."

Bill said, "OK, here goes. Sammy, you get ready to lift Dusty."

Dave called, "Wait a minute!

Someone hold his head and keep him calm!"

Kathy held him and kept talking to him. The dog lay still. Only his eyes seemed alive.

Bill said, "Wait. I've got on two jackets. I'm taking off my windbreaker. Look, it's lined, so it's warm. And it has strings that tie at the bottom.

"I can fix it like a big bag to carry him in."

He pulled the strings as tight as they would go. He tied them together.

He laid the windbreaker on the ground with the zipper still open.

He said, "Sammy, lay Dusty in it when we get him free."

Then he stepped on the metal bar.

He said, "NOW!"

Everyone moved fast.

Kathy and Sammy picked Dusty up

and lowered him into the windbreaker.

Mrs. Tandy zipped it up.

Then Bill took his foot off the bar. The trap snapped shut ... but only on thin air.

Dusty was free.

But now his eyes were closed.

Sammy asked, "Is he dead, Kathy?"

Chapter 6:
Skin and Bones

Kathy said, "He's alive, Sammy.   I can feel his heart beating.

"But his leg looks terrible.   It's as skinny as a stick.   And it's hanging all bent near the bottom.

"The foot doesn't look like it will ever work again."

Only Dusty's head showed outside of Bill's windbreaker.

Sammy put his arms under the dog. He carried him up to the snowmobiles.

Mrs. Tandy said, "Will you be warm enough, Bill?"

Bill nodded. "Sure. This other jacket's really thick.

"But we have to figure out how to get Dusty down the mountain. How can we keep him safe on the snowmobile?"

Dave asked, "Is he very heavy?"

Bill shook his head. "He's all skin and bones. I bet he doesn't even weigh thirty pounds."

Dave said, "Then Kathy can get on the snowmobile with Bill. Kathy, you're small enough to ride in front with Dusty

46

while Bill drives.

"Is that OK with you? You could tie the arms of the windbreaker around your neck."

Kathy said, "Sure … that'll work. Dusty can just hang in front of me, in Bill's jacket."

Dave said, "Hold him steady with one arm. But hold tight to the snowmobile with the other hand.

"That's the way. Think you can keep him there?"

Kathy said, "Don't worry. I won't let go of him for a second."

Mrs. Tandy said, "Be sure to let us know if you start to get tired. We can stop and let you rest."

With Dave leading, they started back down the zig-zag trail.

Kathy's arm was tired by the time they got to the first turn in the path.

But she didn't say a word.

She just held the dog safe and changed arms.

All the way down the mountain she felt Dusty's warm breath beneath her chin.

Dave drove very slowly.

It took over an hour to get back to the ranch.

Mr. and Mrs. Adams came out to the yard, waving and shouting hello.

Then Mrs. Adams noticed the bag-like thing in front of Kathy.

She said, "My goodness, what do you have there?"

Bill un-tied the windbreaker from around Kathy's neck.

Sammy was already off his snowmobile.

He said, "We've GOT him!"

Dave said, "It's Dusty. We found Dusty. In a trap. He's barely alive, and he's hurt, bad."

Mr. and Mrs. Adams could hardly speak.

Mr. Adams's voice shook when he said, "Quick, bring him into the kitchen."

He said to Mrs. Adams, "Let's lay some old towels on the little couch, Ella. We need to make him comfortable."

Kathy took Dusty out of the windbreaker.

They all helped put him down on the towels.

Mr. and Mrs. Adams looked at their dog and cried like babies.

Mr. Adams went to the phone and called the vet.

They heard him say, "It's an emergency, Kate, or I wouldn't ask you to drive up in all that snow.

"I need you to come to my place, right away. We found our dog. He's been gone a month. He's in terrible shape."

Then Mr. Adams called the caretaker's

cabin. He said, "Ed, you're not going to believe this.

"The Woodlanders found Dusty. He was in a trap that the owner never bothered to check.

"He's still alive.

"Yes, Kate's on the way."

Then he hung up and turned to everyone. "I'm calling the sheriff now. There's a law against setting traps and not checking them.

"Animals can suffer for weeks, just like Dusty did."

Mr. Adams put in the call.

Sheriff Garza answered from his car. He was just a few miles away. He said he would head for the ranch.

Just then Ed opened the kitchen door. He was a tall man with a friendly face.

He said hello to the Woodlanders, but walked on past them to the couch.

When he looked down at the dog, his face turned stormy.

He said, "I don't believe it! Alive all this time.

"Fighting for his life, alone, for a month. And all for nothing!

"If I ever get my hands on whoever set that trap ... "

Sammy said, "Wait a minute. What do you mean, all for nothing?

"He's alive, isn't he?

"He can get better, can't he?"

Ed said, "Looks to me like the lower part of his back leg will never be good again. It's dead and rotten. The leg will have to be cut off.

"And he's starved nearly dead.

"Probably the kindest thing would be ... to have the vet put him to sleep."

Sammy said, "Put him to sleep? KILL him, you mean? KILL him after he tried to stay alive for a month?

"And ate nothing but raw deer?

"And almost froze to death eating snow?

"And had his leg caught all that time?

"And now you say the vet should KILL him?"

Before anyone could stop him, Sammy lowered his head like a goat.

He butted Ed right in the stomach.

Chapter 7:
Sheriff Garza

Ed almost fell over backward.

Mr. Adams caught him.

Bill grabbed Sammy and pulled him across the room.

Mrs. Tandy said, "I'm SO sorry, Ed. I hope he didn't hurt you."

Ed said, "No ... well, just a little. Not any more than a wild billy goat. That's one strong young fellow! 'Specially his head!"

Sammy was red in the face. He felt bad. Ed had been so nice to him last summer.

He muttered, "I'm sorry I butted you."

Ed said, "And I'm sorry I said that in front of you, Sammy."

Mr. Adams said, "Well, there is some truth in what you said, Ed. I know you love Dusty, too.

"I know you don't want him to have extra pain ... if he's going to die anyway."

Ed said, "That's it, Abe. I've spent the last three winters with Dusty. This dog is like my baby."

56

He held his hand near Dusty's nose. Dusty's eyes were closed, but he sniffed a little.

Then his tongue gave Ed's hand a quick lick.

Now ED'S eyes filled with tears.

Kathy was the first to do something that made sense.

She ran to the sink. In a minute she came back with a wet dish cloth and a glass of warm water.

She squeezed drops of water out of the cloth and into Dusty's half-open mouth.

Mrs. Adams wiped her eyes. She said, "That's the idea. Let's stop blubbering ... and figure out what to do to help Dusty."

Mrs. Tandy said, "Why not give him a little white bread? Maybe wet it down with chicken soup."

Kathy said, "Food might not be a good thing for Dusty right now.

Especially if he needs an operation on that leg. We should wait till the vet gets here."

Then the vet came.

Mr. Adams said, "Kate, thanks so much for coming. These are the folks who found our Dusty. Folks, this is Dr. Kate Miller.

"The dog's right over here, Kate."

The vet looked carefully at Dusty's hurt leg.

She said, "I'm sorry. The leg will have to be taken off.

"He's weak, but there's a chance, a small chance, that he may pull through.

"I've seen dogs with three legs live long, happy lives.

"He will need a lot of care for the next week ... water ... hand-feeding ... medicines ... bandages ... and later on, a bath."

Dave said, "Kathy's better than anyone at bandages, and giving medicine."

Kathy looked at Dave and blushed.

Sammy said, "She's going to be a doctor ... she's pretty brainy. But I can help, too!

"I can be in charge of feeding him. I'll stay up all night if I have to. Count on me. I know all about food."

Then he lifted his shirt and patted his round stomach. It sounded like a little drum.

Mr. Adams smiled for the first time

since he'd seen Dusty.

Just then a car drove up.

Mrs. Adams said, "Sheriff Garza's here."

In walked a short, strong-looking man. The sheriff stepped over to the couch. His eyes rested on the bony dog.

He looked around at everyone.

He growled, "We are going to catch the crook who did this. Now first, who found the poor animal?"

Mr. Adams said, "These five, Mike. They're the Woodlanders, friends of mine ... Becky Tandy, Dave Briggs, Bill, Kathy, and Sammy Westburg.

"And you know Kate!

"Folks, this is our sheriff, Mike Garza."

The sheriff said, "Glad to meet you. I'm wondering, can you show me where you found this trap?"

Bill said, "Sure! Not one trap, but two, pretty close together. But do you know how to drive a snowmobile?"

The sheriff said, "Well, I haven't in a while. But I can learn again mighty fast!"

Mrs. Tandy said, "There's no need. You can ride with me."

Dave said, "Sammy and Bill can ride together. Kathy, you come on with me."

Kathy looked pleased, but she said, "I think maybe I should stay with Dusty."

Kate said, "No, you won't have to.

I've already given him a shot so he won't feel any pain.

"He will sleep for several hours.

"I'm going to work on that leg right here. He's so weak, I'm afraid to chance moving him.

"By the time you get back, he will just be waking up.

"Then you can start taking care of him."

The sheriff said, "Come on, everybody. I'm going to need all the help I can get to solve this. And believe me, I'm not going to stop until I do!"

He turned to Mr. Adams. "Abe, I'll need a big bolt cutter from you. I'll have to cut those traps off their chains."

Sammy said, "Wait just a minute. Don't start yet! I'm starving."

Mrs. Adams said, "Take what you want from the kitchen, child. I'll help you." ·

They threw some sandwiches together and sat down.

Sammy gobbled half a sandwich. Then he gobbled the other half.

Bill whispered, "You're sucking that in like a vacuum cleaner! DisGUSTing!"

Sammy whispered back, "And you're talking with your mouth full. MORE disGUSTing!"

They finished and hurried out to the snowmobiles.

The sheriff got on behind Mrs. Tandy.

Sammy whispered to Bill, "Mrs. T.'s got a new boyfriend!"

Bill said, "Just because they're riding together? I suppose that means they're married, too."

Sammy made his poison-spider face at Bill. He said, "Come on! Let's start! Don't sit here talking! Let's go catch that crook!"

Chapter 8:
Tennessee Turner

Up the mountain they roared.

They didn't stop until they reached the traps.

With gloved hands, the sheriff emptied

the one that held the dead deer. He turned the trap over.

Then he said, "WAIT! I KNOW THIS TRAP! I know who owns it!"

Dave called from his snowmobile, "Aren't traps pretty much alike? How can you tell who owns that one?"

The sheriff said, "Because I mark any illegal trap that we pick up."

Kathy said, "What makes a trap illegal?"

The sheriff said, "Well, in this case, not checking the trap soon enough after setting it.

"A year ago we caught this guy doing the same thing with this very trap. His name was Tennessee Turner."

Sammy said, "That's a weird name. Why is he called that?"

Sheriff Garza said, "Because every time someone does something, he says, 'Back in Tennessee we do it different.'

"In fact, when we caught him last year, he said our laws were no good.

"He said, 'Back in Tennessee, people can trap any way they please. Back there we know animals were put on earth for skinning and eating.'

"He said animals caught in traps don't feel pain. He claimed their legs get numb right away."

Sammy yelled, "I know what's numb! His SKULL is numb!

"But not because he's from Tennessee. It's because ... because ... he's mean!"

The sheriff said, "Well, the judge hit Tennessee Turner with a big fine. I thought Turner would change his ways after that.

"Before we returned his traps, I scratched this mark on all of them."

The sheriff pointed. There was the

mark "TT" on the bottom of the trap.

He let Bill and Sammy cut the chain on the other trap.

He put the traps into plastic bags. Mrs. Tandy helped him tie them to the snowmobiles.

Then Sheriff Garza said, "No use looking for other clues here. I don't see any footprints except ours.

"Let's get down to the ranch and do some planning. It will be almost dark by the time we get there."

As soon as they got back, they went to check on Dusty.

He was on the couch.

He was lying very still and breathing deeply.

The vet was gone.

Mrs. Adams said, "Dusty's in better shape than Kate could believe. She thinks maybe he might make it."

Mr. Adams added, "But the poor thing is worn out! He will probably sleep for a little while longer. And Ed's gone back to his cabin."

Sheriff Garza said, "Well, then, this is a good time to talk. I want to tell you what I'm thinking.

"My team will start looking for Turner.

"I know some places where he used to rent rooms, so I can check those.

"But I have a special job for you snowmobilers."

Dave asked, "What is it?"

Sheriff Garza said, "Once in a while Turner uses an old hunting cabin. It's way up in the highest mountain meadow.

"It doesn't belong to him. It belongs to another hunter.

"He just breaks into it and camps there sometimes.

"I'd be much obliged if you'd take a look at the place."

Sammy said, "Oh, boy! What if we find it, and he's in it? I'll jump on him, and drag him down to you!"

70

The sheriff said, "Oh, no, my boy. If you find him, pretend you're just out for a joy ride.

"Then hurry back down and phone me right away."

Bill said, "We have ten days before we go home. Is there anything else we can do?"

The sheriff said, "Well, just south of where you found the traps ... there's another place you might check first.

"The cabin belongs to an older couple.

"Now, there's no path to it.

"But remember that rocky cliff ... right above where you found the traps?

"Follow it south about half a mile.

"You'll come to a little log cabin, right up against the cliff.

"Talk to the folks who own it. Maybe they've seen Turner."

Dave said, "You mean someone lives

up there ALL YEAR ROUND?"

Sammy said, "People with BRAINS?"

Bill poked him.

The sheriff said, "You bet. In a tiny one-room place.

"Snow covers the roof every year.

"Sometimes even the walls.

"Two real old-timers live there. Jess and Lena Webb."

Mrs. Tandy said, "That must be hard, living up there alone. How do they get food?"

Sheriff Garza said, "Jess and Lena may be old, but they get around. Every year Jess shoots a couple of deer, and maybe a bear.

"He and Lena cut the meat into strips. Then they hang it outside on wooden racks.

"Then the meat dries, like beef jerky. Only it's deer jerky. Or bear jerky."

Kathy said, "But how do they get other things they need?"

The sheriff said, "Well, they pan the streams for gold!

"Then they carry it all the way into town and sell it. With the money they buy coffee, sugar, flour, and whatever else they need."

Sammy shouted, "THEY PAN FOR GOLD? Forget the hunting cabin!

"We are going to Jess and Lena's cabin! TOMORROW!"

Chapter 9:
The Missing Cabin

Just at that moment they heard "Yip!"
   They looked over to the couch.
   Dusty was awake!
   He was lying down, but he had his

head up.

Sheriff Garza said, "Look at that animal! He lost a leg. He nearly lost his life. He's as skinny as a willow twig. But he's trying to wag his tail!"

Mr. and Mrs. Adams invited the sheriff to stay for chicken and rice.

Sammy joked, "Hey, this is just what Dusty had for dinner! We are eating dog food!"

Dave said, "Good! That's what we SHOULD be eating. Tomorrow we have to be hunting dogs, and track down our man."

The next morning the boys woke up to a tapping sound. It was Kathy tapping on the wall between their rooms.

Dave tapped back.

While they got dressed, Bill said, "You know, we should all learn Morse code.

Then we could tap out sentences to each other."

Dave said, "I know Morse code. I learned it from a library book."

Sammy moaned, "You read EVERY-thing. I'll NEVER catch up with you."

Dave said, "You don't have to catch up with me! I can teach you guys a Morse code signal in a second. Listen, it goes like this … "

He tapped three times close together.

Then he made three slow taps.

Then he tapped three times close together again.

77

Bill and Sammy tried it.

Tap, tap, tap.

Tap ... tap ... tap.

Tap, tap, tap.

Sammy said, "Now that I know it, what does it mean?"

Bill said, "I know what it means. It's the signal that ships use. It's the letters S-O-S."

Sammy asked, "Why do they spell out S-O-S? I would use H-E-L-P. Does S-O-S stand for HELP in some other language?"

Dave said, "Some people think it stands for SAVE OUR SHIP, but that's not true. Three dots and three dashes and three dots are just easy to remember."

Sammy yelled, "S-O-S!"

Bill said, "What?"

Sammy said, "SAVE OUR SAMMY! From starving! Let's go eat breakfast!"

Laughing, they went to meet the

others in the kitchen.

Dusty wagged his tail when he saw them.

They all patted his thin body.

Bill said, "He feels like furry cloth lying over some sticks."

Sammy said, "I wish I could give him some of my extra fat. I have plenty!"

Kathy smoothed Dusty's fur and said, "You brave old thing. I know you'll get better. You HAVE to get better."

They fed him some more chicken and rice.

Soon Dusty stopped eating and fell into a deep sleep.

So they ate breakfast and helped clean up.

Then Mrs. Adams handed Mrs. Tandy a big cloth bag.

She said, "Sandwiches for lunch! That way you folks will be free to hunt for

Tennessee Turner all day.

"We won't look for you until mid-afternoon."

Everyone thanked her. They got onto their snowmobiles, with Dave in the lead.

They zoomed up the mountain, going higher and higher with each turn.

Finally they reached the place where the traps had been.

Dave pulled to a stop.

He said, "Now I'm going slowly from here on. I'll lead you along the cliff, like the sheriff said."

Mrs. Tandy said, "Fine. That way we can watch for any sign of Turner. And we can watch for other traps, and footprints, too."

Kathy said, "And maybe Jess or Lena will be outside. Let's watch for them on the way."

They went along for a long time, driving, stopping, looking, listening.

They came to one place where they had to move away from the cliff wall.

A giant snow hill stuck out from it.

But they still couldn't find the cabin.

Bill said, "We must have come a half a mile along this cliff. Maybe more. We should have seen the cabin by now."

Dave said, "Seems like that to me, too. But we haven't. So on we go."

They drove along the cliff for quite a while longer.

By then it was 11:00.

Sammy looked disappointed.

He wrinkled his forehead. He pouted.

Finally he mumbled, "I guess we aren't going to discover ANYthing! Some hunting dogs! I bet we are LOST!"

Chapter 10:
Space Monsters

Kathy said, "Do you think we got our directions wrong?"

Sammy said, "Maybe Sheriff Garza meant we should go along the TOP of the cliff. And he told us below by mistake."

Dave shook his head. "There's something wrong or we would have found the cabin by now.

"The sheriff wouldn't have given us bad directions."

Bill said, "Well, we probably should start back. Look how dark the sky is."

Sammy was so cold, he was shaking.

He said, "Boy, it looks awful. And it's getting colder. I feel like we are on the moon or something."

Mrs. Tandy said, "Look how gray the snow looks without the sunshine.

"And how blue the shadows are."

Sammy added, "I bet Mars looks just like this up close."

Dave said, "Well, I guess we should turn around. Let's ride back for about an hour. By then it will be noon, and time for lunch."

Mrs. Tandy said, "How about if we stop on the side of that snow hill we passed? Maybe it would protect us from the wind while we eat."

So they rode back through the gloomy cold, to the hill against the cliff.

They ate while they sat on their snowmobiles.

Soon everyone but Kathy was munching on corn chips.

Suddenly she said, "Hey, what's that noise?"

Dave said, "What noise?"

She said, "I hear sort of a dull pounding noise."

Sammy said, "You're hearing things, Kathy."

She shook her head. "No, listen."

Then they all heard it.

Thud, thud, thud.

Sammy whispered, "It's coming from inside the hill. Do you know what it is? I'll TELL you!

"I KNEW it looked weird up here. Like the moon. Or Mars. It's space monsters! Let's get out of here!"

Bill grabbed his arm. He said, "Wait a second, Sammy. Don't panic."

Sammy said, "What do you mean, don't panic! You think we should wait around here and get eaten alive?

"Don't you remember that monster movie last week?

"Those gross space birds landed in the mountains and started to dig inside it!

"They had that one entire mountain hollowed out!

"Don't you remember? They attacked the rest of the Earth from their mountain hide-out!

"They were disgusting giant hairy woodpeckers! Blood-colored! And they ate people. Pecked right through them!

"Don't panic? Let me go! I'M OUT OF HERE!"

Bill said, "STOP. You know that wasn't real."

Sammy said, "Well, that NOISE we just heard was real."

Everyone was feeling a little strange by then. Sammy's fear was getting to them.

They listened carefully.

This time they heard ...

Thud, thud, thud.

Thud ... thud ... thud.

Thud, thud, thud.

And they heard what sounded like a voice coming from inside the hill.

"EL! EH-UH-OW! EL!"

Sammy said, "It IS a voice from outer space! It doesn't even speak our language!"

Bill pulled Sammy off the snowmobile.

He said, "Listen, Sammy. Stop scaring everybody, and listen!"

They heard it again.

Thud, thud, thud.

Thud ... thud ... thud.

Thud, thud, thud.

Sammy said, "That's a giant woodpecker beak! Or some weird machine!"

Bill looked excited. "I know what

those thuds are! It's Dave's famous S-O-S!
Three dots. Three dashes. Three dots.
Whoever it is needs help!"

The voice came through again.

"EL! EH-UH-OW! EL!"

Not one voice. Two voices.

Dave said, "There are people inside the
hill! They're yelling and banging, but
the snow's blocking the sound!"

Kathy looked puzzled. "How could
someone be inside a hill?"

Mrs. Tandy said, "Unless ... it's not a
hill."

Bill shouted, "WAIT! It must be the
cabin in there!"

89

Sammy said, "No way! How would it get under all that snow?"

Dave pointed up the mountain side. "There's your answer."

They saw a bare strip running forty feet up.

Bill said, "A snow slide! There was a snow slide!

"Something shook the snow loose. A bear. A falling tree. Something. And all the snow dumped down on the house!"

Suddenly Kathy shouted, "AIR! They're probably running out of air!"

Bill ran up to the front of the hill. He started kicking and digging into the snow with his hands and feet.

Dave said, "Hold off for a minute. Let me see something." He took a good look.

"Above the snow slide the mountain

goes back flat. I don't think any more snow will slide down." The others started digging with Bill.

Dave said, "Kathy, this time we HAVE to split up! Grab a snowmobile! "We've got to go down the mountain for help.

"We need shovels. And Mr. Adams! We have to get Jess and Lena out before the air's gone."

He called to the others, "Take turns digging, so you don't get tired. It may take us a while to get back."

Then he and Kathy raced off down the mountain.

Chapter 11:
Big! And Fat! And Hairy!

An hour and a half had gone by.

At last the sound of motors broke through the mountain air.

Snowmobiles were coming.

Sammy, Bill, and Mrs. Tandy were still digging in the snow with their icy mittens.

Dave pulled up to the cabin. Kathy and Mr. Adams were right behind him with the shovels.

They dug to the door in only a few minutes.

Bill called, "We've cleared it! Jess! Lena! You can come out!"

The door pushed open, and out walked ... TWO MONSTER THINGS!

They were BIG! And FAT! And HAIRY!

Sammy yelled, "YIKES!" He ran behind Bill and held on to him.

Then he stuck his head out for another look.

The monster things' heads were covered with black ski masks and scarves and big fur hats. Only their eyes showed.

94

Each thing had a huge bear head hanging forward, next to its own head.

The bear paws met in front, beneath the bear head.

Sammy whispered, "Look at those claws. They could KILL you!"

But then he noticed that the monsters had on leather boots. Regular old leather boots.

And then one of them spoke. It said, "Thanks for the rescue!"

It reached an arm out and shook Bill's hand.

It said, "Lucky for us we had these bearskins in the cabin.

"And lucky for us that you came along! We've been without heat since around six this morning.

"Had to put the fire out when the snow covered the chimney."

The other one said, "We've got on almost every piece of clothing we own!

"I'm Lena. And this is Jess, my husband.

"Can't tell you how grateful we are to you.

"We could have died here, and frozen stiff as jerky.

"You look awful, Jess. And I must look the same.

"Say, did we scare you clean out of your skins when we came out?"

Sammy jumped out from behind Bill. He said, "Oh, no. I knew it was you the whole time. Who else could you be ... SPACE MONSTERS?"

He laughed as if he had told a really great joke.

Bill whispered to him, "Then why were you hiding behind my back?"

Sammy whispered back, "Quiet, blabbermouth. I wasn't hiding. I was keeping you warm."

Lena said, "Well, this space monster wishes we could get the fire going again."

Bill put an arm around Sammy and Kathy.

He said, "We three can climb up on the roof. We have shovels. We can cut steps in the snow up there ... and clear the snow off the chimney.

"You'll be able to start a fire in a minute!"

First they carried Dave from the snowmobile to a chair in the cabin.

Then they climbed up to the roof and got to work.

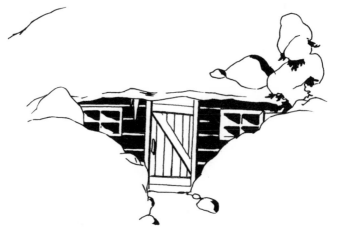

Ten minutes later Jess and Mr. Adams had a hot fire going.

Soon they were all snug and warm.

Jess and Lena took off their bearskins ...

coonskin hats

scarves

ski masks
leather boots
outer jackets
inner jackets
... and two sweaters each.

And there stood two smiling people.

The others took off their warm clothes, too.

Jess said, "What can we do to thank you for saving us?"

Sammy said, "You can show us how to pan for gold, that's what!"

Mr. Adams said, "Well, first things first. Jess, Lena, we should explain what's going on.

"The Woodlanders here were helping me out. See, my dog Dusty got caught in an illegal trap. For a month.

"He lost his leg and may not live. We are all trying to find the guy who set the trap. Tennessee Turner."

Lena said, "Tennessee Turner! Why, we know that fellow.

"He came by here hungry last fall. Never asked for food. Stole some of our meat from the drying rack.

"I wasn't gone more than two minutes. When I got back, I saw him running off through the trees. Had on snowshoes."

Jess said, "A few weeks later, though, he left half a deer at our front door.

"We guessed right away it came from him. It was a lot more meat than he took, by a long sight."

Lena said, "Seems like he isn't bad clear through. But wild and selfish."

Mrs. Tandy said, "Well, his wildness nearly killed Dusty."

Jess said, "Say, looks like you all saved my life just in time today. Because I know right where Turner is spending this spring.

"He's in the mountain meadows, in a hunting cabin.   I can take you there tomorrow morning.

"But for today, Lena and I owe you a thank-you party.   Since it's too late to keep searching for Turner, let's get started partying!"

Chapter 12:
A Party

Mr. Adams said, "First I'll help you re-hang your cabin door, Jess. Let's swing it inward, so you're never trapped inside again."

The Woodlanders worked with them.

Then Jess asked, "Now where's that old tin tub? The one with the hole in it."

Lena said, "Jess Webb! Why would you want that worn-out, no-good tub?"

But she started moving boxes away from the cabin wall.

Behind them she found a big, round washtub.

Jess pointed to the hole in it. He said, "It won't hold water anymore, but I knew it would come in handy some day!"

Lena said, "You silly old coot. What's it good for?"

Jess smiled. "You'll see. The first part of this party is going to be sledding!

"Anyone who wants to sled can sit in this tub and slide down the hill above us!"

Kathy, Sammy, Bill, and Mrs. Tandy looked at the tub. In a minute they had

their warm clothes back on.   Mr. Adams
joined them.

They ran outside.   Sammy climbed up
the snow-covered house.   He pulled the
tub along with him.

He stepped inside the tub and said,
"Give me a push-off, Bill."

But then he wiggled.

He went spinning around and down
without a push!

Halfway down he hit a lump of snow.

He tipped over. He slid down to the flat ground.

The tub slid down by itself.

Sammy pulled it back up the hill.

He said, "I get another turn! I spilled out!"

But Bill just grabbed the tub and jumped in.

He made it farther than Sammy, but he dumped over, too.

Kathy tried it next.

Sammy said, "Wait, let me in first, Kathy. You sit on my lap and I'll show you how to do it."

Bill laughed and said, "Sure, you'll show her how to get spilled out!"

That started a snowball fight, so Mrs. Tandy and Mr. Adams tried the tub sled.

Inside the cabin Dave was busy looking around and talking with the Webbs.

Jess showed him a beautiful patch work quilt.

He said, "Lena and I made this together! And we both sew on buttons and patch our clothes, like old-time sailors did."

Lena said, "And we whittle, too!"

She showed Dave a chain, carved from one piece of wood.

When the others came back in, Lena pointed to a round iron stove. She said, "I heated up water for hot chocolate. And we can make popcorn!"

She took a big iron kettle off the top of the stove.

She poured steaming-hot water into eight tin mugs with cocoa powder and powdered milk.

They drank it while they made the popcorn.

Lena put the corn into a box made of metal and screen.

They took turns shaking the box back and forth in the fireplace.

The corn began to pop.

Pop, pop, pop.

Pop... pop ... pop.

Sammy said, "That sounds like MORE Morse code!"

Bill poked Sammy and whispered, "Hey, maybe the popcorn is really tiny space guys. Carrying messages from outer space."

Sammy hit him on the arm.

Finally Mr. Adams said, "Jess, Lena, this was a great party.

"But we have to get down the mountain before it gets dark.

"I'm going to borrow two more snowmobiles from my neighbor.

"Tomorrow morning we six ... and the sheriff ... will stop by.

"Would you really help us find Tennessee Turner?"

Lena said, "Of course we will!"

They all waved good-bye and piled outside.

Mr. Adams carried Dave to the snowmobile.

Bill said to Sammy, "Lucky thing those space monsters didn't eat us."

He got a face full of snow as an answer. But he didn't care. He was already thinking about tomorrow.

Chapter 13:
The Last Trap

It was early morning.

Five snowmobiles stopped at the Jess and Lena's cabin.

Riding them were Sheriff Garza, the

Woodlanders, and Mr. Adams.

When Jess and Lena joined them, they all headed up the mountain.

In two hours they reached the snow-covered meadow. It sparkled with diamonds of sunlight.

Then they came to an old wooden hunting shack.

The sheriff knocked on the door.

No answer.

He knocked again.

No answer.

Then they heard a sound coming from the back of the shack.

They dashed around.

They saw a man running away!

All he had on were boots and long underwear.

He was carrying a jacket. He tried to get his arms into it as he ran.

He disappeared into the thick woods.

Sheriff   Garza   shouted,   "STOP,
TENNESSEE!   It's the sheriff!"

But the man kept running.

The sheriff said, "He's not armed.

"Jess and Lena, go wait with Dave.

"Now, let's get him!"

They all raced after Turner, with Bill
and Sammy in the lead.

Turner was fast, and he had a head
start.   But Sammy and Bill were as
strong as a couple of mountain ponies.

113

They tailed him as he crashed through the bushes.

And then, suddenly, they heard a scream of pain.

It rang across the meadow and bounced off the mountaintops.

They could still hear its echo as they caught up with Turner.

He was down in the snow.

He lay twisting and turning and moaning and crying.

He was trying to pull off the thing that held his foot.

It was a TRAP! He was caught in the jaws of one of his own traps ... another one that he had set and forgotten about.

He screamed, and then cried, "Help! Help! Get this thing off me!"

Sammy and Bill got some branches and carefully poked the snow in front of them to check for traps.

When they reached Tennessee, Bill said, "Grab his shoulders, Sammy. When I open the trap, pull."

Bill stood on the trap's metal bar. He forced its jaws open.

Sammy used all his strength to drag Turner out.

The man moaned a few more times. Then he passed out.

Bill shouted, "Over here! We've got him! But be careful! Walk in our footsteps!"

The sheriff, Mr. Adams, Mrs. Tandy, and Kathy broke through the bushes.

Kathy saw the man was badly hurt.

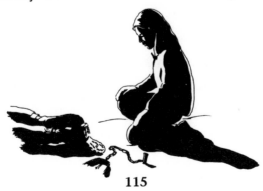

115

She said, "Sheriff, we have to get his jacket onto him. And someone has to go to the cabin for some blankets."

Sheriff Garza and Mr. Adams ran to the cabin. As they rushed back they heard a snowmobile coming.

Dave was picking his way through the woods on it.

He said, "Put him on my lap. It will be a tight squeeze, with the seat built up like it is. But I can get him back to the cabin."

They wrapped him in blankets and lifted him onto Dave's lap.

Turner moaned with pain.

At the hunting cabin they got ready for the trip down.

Mr. Adams, who was best with the snowmobiles, took Tennessee Turner with him.

Kathy rode with Dave, her arms

around his strong chest.

Mrs. Tandy rode behind Sheriff Garza.

Sammy took Jess.

Bill drove Lena.

They dropped off Jess and Lena at their cabin and started for the ranch.

Half the time Turner moaned with pain. Half the time he was passed out.

They drove right up to the sheriff's car at the ranch.

Then the sheriff drove Turner down to the hospital.

Later that day the Woodlanders and Mr. and Mrs. Adams set off on the snowmobiles.

They came to Jess and Lena's cabin and knocked on the door.

Jess opened it.

There the seven of them were, their arms full of packages.

Lena said, "Jess, you old fool. Why didn't you say company was coming?"

Jess said, "I didn't know they were! Don't stand there scolding me like a squirrel. Let's find them something to eat!"

Mrs. Adams said, "No need. We brought YOU a little something to eat.

"I started to worry, waiting for Abe and the rest.

"And when I worry, I cook up a storm!

"So look in these packages. I made us a whole party!

"Ed's looking after Dusty, so we all could come along and help eat it."

Mr. Adams said, "We have something to celebrate, too. Turner won't be trapping ever again. Not even in season."

Sammy said, "Hooray! So, what's holding up the party? Here are turkey

sandwiches, and milk, and apples, and pies, and about a thousand cookies."

He stuffed half a turkey sandwich in his mouth, and was quiet for a minute. Then everyone dug into the food.

They talked and laughed and ate until it was time to go.

Then they said good-bye to Lena and Jess and the hill of snow.

The Woodlanders and their friends headed back to the ranch.

When they walked into the kitchen, Dusty wagged his tail hello.

119

His tail hit the floor.

Thump, thump, thump.

Thump ... thump ... thump.

Thump, thump, thump.

Sammy shouted, "He's spelling out S-O-S! Well, don't worry, Dusty old boy, we WILL help you get better!"